Riddles
by a
J.R.R. Tolkien Fan

Written by

Pam Jones

Riddles by a J.R.R. Tolkien Fan
written by Pam Jones

© Pam and Taff Jones
http://www.pamandtaffjones.com

Published with the permission, but not approval,
of The J.R.R. Tolkien Estate Ltd.

Riddles by Pam Jones
Design © 131 Design Ltd
www.131design.org
Published by Tricorn Books 2013
www.tricornbooks.co.uk

All rights reserved. No part of this publication may be reproduced, stored in any retrieval system or transmitted in any form or by any means, electronic, mechanical, photocopying, recording or otherwise, without the prior written permission of the copyright holder for which application should be addressed in the first instance to the publishers. No liability shall be attached to the authors, the copyright holder or the publishers for loss or damage of any nature suffered as a result of the reliance on the reproduction of any of the contents of this publication or any errors or omissions in the contents.

A CIP catalogue record for this book is available from
The British Library.
ISBN 978-1-909660-05-2
Published 2013 by Tricorn Books,
a trading name of 131 Design Ltd.
131 High Street, Old Portsmouth, PO1 2HW
Printed & bound by Berforts in the UK

Composed of wood, with many leaves
Attached to spine, instead of branch
Yet not a breath, will it exhale
Appearing dead, to untrained eyes

Book

Magic I possess
I glow when I'm near Orcs
Made by skilful Elves
I'm Bilbo's famous sword

Sting

*It goes well with cheese and bread
Has a good nose as well
That is sometimes red
But cannot smell*

Wine

A heart with wondrous facets
From the mountain I do stem
Swimming in crystals and gold
Lonely now grey I'm a gem

The Arkenstone

*We are kind folk and easy to fathom
On our birthdays we distribute mathoms
In round houses we consume meals all day
And love spectacular firework displays*

Hobbits (of the Shire)

They possess many frightening eyes
With eight legs which are really scary
And rest in the dark Mirkwood Forest
On massive webs to capture their prey

Giant Spiders

*In the beginning it's alive
Then it's kept all lovely and warm
And it's left for some time to rise
Then once baked it's sliced thin or torn*

Bread

*Some say we're ugly and evil
We dwell beneath the High Pass
In a mountain of dark tunnels
Where it's easy to get lost*

Goblins/Orcs

Immortal, old and kind
By rivers he does dwell
With elven folk in peace
Sage Lord of Rivendell

Elrond

*We have two giant pale eyeses
And get tired of eating fishes
One of us is kind and helpful
The other is dark and spiteful*

Gollum

Deep in the Lonely Mountain I do hide
With friends of jewels and gold I reside
An armoured fire-drake with scales red-gold
Look closer for my weakness if you're bold

Smaug (Dragon)

I'm blue
Tasty
Creamy
Sharp too

Blue Cheese

They speak in their own song
These mighty birds of prey
With piercing long talons
For goblins they do slay

Eagles

*A fire is used to flare me up
So that I can breathe out smoke
Although I'm not a dragon
I'm often used by Shire-folk*

Pipe

Heir of Girion last Lord of Dale
A strong archer with flexible yew bow
Who can translate the song of a thrush
And kill evil with his black arrow

Bard
(The Bowman)

Our favourite game is, to play with rocks
By hurling them to, one another
Or smashing them down, amongst the trees
Echoing across, the mountainsides

Stone Giants

In glistening rich yellows
Shaped rather like bricks
If used as block paving
You'll probably slip

Slabs of Butter

Wise leader of the Council White
A man of skill and Istari
Working with Sauron the Dark Lord
Envious of Gandalf the Grey

Saruman

*I am precious
And made of gold
If you lose me
You will grow old*

The One Ring

*Durin's Folk King
And son of Thrain
A mighty dwarf
With golden chain*

Thorin Oakenshield

Like an umbrella, as a head cap
Too small to protect you from the rain
Found in dark caves or, woods or forests
Juicy in butter, and dry when plain

Mushroom

With long fine hair, and leaf-shaped ears
Graceful, slender and strong are we
We love water and shining stars
And sometimes use, telepathy

Elves

*It's made when you have a sore throat
And it sounds like pony not goat
It can be soothed with herbal teas
Like sweet honey with lemons squeezed*

A Hoarse Voice (like Gollum)

*A skin-changing Northman you'll observe
Who's sometimes bear and sometimes man
By his animals he is served
This mighty Beorning great chieftain*

Beorn

*Mounting our backs we run far and fast
Friends of the goblins we're evil too
We converse in our own dreadful tongue
We'll rip you to shreds if we catch you*

Wargs

*Sometimes I am short and fat
Other times, I'm long and thin
Made of juicy meat I am
Maybe pork, or beef, or lamb*

Sausages

Though we eat mutton fresh
Our favourite is manflesh
From sunlight we will surely flee
Bumbling and stupid giants are we

Trolls

A servant to the king
Remiss Wood-elf and butler
Who's fond of vintage wine
When angry is a growler

Galion

It is deaf and cannot see
Yet has several eyes
Earthy flavours you'll agree
For in the ground it lies

Potato

With grey hair and staff
A tall wise man is he
Who can conjure up great spells
To create peace and harmony

Gandalf

*I am made of butter
Flour and eggs as well
And honey or sugar
I'm tasty to smell*

Cake

Father of Legolas
King of the Silvan Elves
Crowned in woodland flowers
Or red leaves and berries

Thranduil

It has buds but is not a flower
Can whisper, shout loudly, talk even sing
And feels bitter, salty, sweet or sour
Though looks the same whether hobbit or king

Tongue

Dressed in brown and bird tamer
A friend to beasts and birds
More than elves and men
A fool wizard

Radagast the Brown

*Sturdy, short and stocky, are we
With long forked or, braided beards
We love to sing, in harmony
But only when, the pantry's cleared*

Dwarves

It is a globe that does not spin
Is sometimes purple and sometimes green
Has sharp bristly thorns which prick the skin
Yet the hearts can be fried, boiled or steamed

Globe Artichoke

Old raven, the chief
And son of Carc
Messenger by day
And night when dark

Roäc

Leader of Esogarth
And driven moneybags
Selfish and weak in nature
Greedy and large in stature

Master of Lake-town

*Dressed in many bright colours
In nature they're soft and sweet
Yet cannot be spread on bread
Though sound good enough to eat*

Butterflies

*I've hairy toes and wavy hair
With a pantry full of food
Like buttered scones with cream and jam
So can you guess who I am?*

Bilbo Baggins

The End